Henry Addison Nelson

The Divinely Prepared Ruler

Volume 1

Henry Addison Nelson

The Divinely Prepared Ruler
Volume 1

ISBN/EAN: 9783337159092

Printed in Europe, USA, Canada, Australia, Japan

Cover: Foto ©Andreas Hilbeck / pixelio.de

More available books at **www.hansebooks.com**

THE DIVINELY PREPARED RULER,

AND

THE FIT END OF TREASON,

TWO DISCOURSES

DELIVERED AT

THE FIRST PRESBYTERIAN CHURCH,

SPRINGFIELD, ILLINOIS,

BY INVITATION OF THE SESSION,

ON THE

SABBATH FOLLOWING THE BURIAL OF PRESIDENT LINCOLN,

MAY 7, 1865,

BY REV. HENRY A. NELSON,

PASTOR FIRST PRESB'N. CHURCH, ST. LOUIS,

———

SPRINGFIELD, ILLS.:

STEAM PRESS OF BAKER & PHILLIPS,

———

1865.

CORRESPONDENCE.

SPRINGFIELD, ILLS., May 7th, 1865.

REV. H. A. NELSON, D.D.,

St. Louis, Mo.

DEAR SIR: Having had the pleasure of listening to your sermons delivered yesterday in the First Presbyterian Church of this city, and being deeply impressed with the pertinency and truthfulness of the views therein contained; believing, also, that the dissemination of those views at this time cannot fail to be useful, we respectfully request a copy of each for publication.

Yours, truly,

R. OFFICER,
JOHN WILLIAMS,
JACOB BUNN,
S. H. MELVIN,
J. W. LANE,
B. F. FOX,
G. JAYNE,
FRANK W. TRACY,
W. H. HAYDEN,
H. B. BUCK.

ST. LOUIS, May 9, 1865.

GENTLEMEN:

I deemed it a precious privilege, on the Sabbath after we laid the body of our murdered President in the tomb, to preach to a large concourse of his former neighbors, in the church in which he used to worship. I felt the responsibility to be very great, and am much comforted by your assurance that it was discharged acceptably.

The views which I expressed, and of which you speak approvingly, are essentially the same which are uttered from thousands of pulpits, and platforms, and presses all over our land, and all round the world. I can, however, imagine that discourses privileged to be delivered, *at that place and time*, may have an interest which they owe to that circumstance, quite independent of their own merit. Just as the pictures of Mr. LINCOLN's modest home in your city, and of the horse that drew his family carriage, or even a sprig or leaf plucked near his tomb must now be precious to all who can possess them, so I can imagine that many may like to read discourses occasioned by his death, and delivered so near his tomb, so soon after it received his remains. If this should give them a currency which they would not otherwise have; if thus they can (as you suggest) be the means of disseminating truthful and pertinent views on the subjects of which they treat, I ought not to withhold them from circulation.

Gentlemen: You and the people of Springfield, whom you represent, have a most enviable privilege. You are the favored guardians of a tomb which will be visited by tens of thousands of your countrymen, and by the lovers of virtue and liberty from all other lands. You are entrusted by your country with the keeping, for her and for mankind, of the most revered form that has walked the earth in this century. I thank you, gentlemen, for the honor you do me, in giving my humble advocacy of LINCOLN's principles this grateful association with LINCOLN's tomb.

HENRY A. NELSON.

To R. Officer, John Williams, Jacob Bunn, and others.

THE DIVINELY PREPARED RULER.

--- -- - --

Ps. 78: 70—72—"He chose David also his servant, and took him from the sheep-folds; from following the ewes great with young he brought him to feed Jacob his people, and Israel his inheritance.

So he fed them according to the integrity of his heart, and guided them by the skillfulness of his hands."

This text brings prominently before us that remarkable divine election and providence whereby David was brought from the humble circumstances and occupations of a peasant, to the high position and responsibilities of a monarch. It also suggests a connection between the pursuits of his early life and the noble character exemplified in his eventful and glorious reign.

The appropriateness of these topics to this occasion is manifest. We mourn for one whom God chose to rule a great people during a most wonderful, most critical, most glorious period of their history, and whom He trained for that great work in an early life, not unlike that which formed and developed the mind and body of king David.

When David is first introduced, in the scripture history, (1 Sam. xvi,) we behold him a bright and handsome boy, "ruddy and of a beautiful countenance," according to the simple and graphic Bible phrase. He comes in from the pastures, where he has been keeping the flock of his father,

into the presence of the "man of God," who has been sent
to Bethlehem, to anoint one from among the sons of Jesse,
to be the reprobate Saul's successor to the throne of Israel.
Samuel's prophetic insight recognizes, in the ruddy strip-
ling, the elect of God to that high office, and signifies that
divine designation by anointing him with oil. God accom-
panies the external symbol, which He has ordered, with
such bestowment of His own Spirit as is needful to rouse,
to quicken, and thenceforth to direct the before latent roy-
alty of young David's soul. From that time, as we follow
his steps in the thrilling record, along the adventurous and
eventful track of his life, we are continually sensible of the
presence of truest nobility. All that can be expressed by
the epithets *heroic*, *princely*, *royal*, is habitually exemplified. The few instances of unworthy, unmanly, even criminal behavior, (which are by no means to be disguised or
extenuated,) are felt to be exceptional, in strange and vio-
lent contrast with the prevailing character, which still,
notwithstanding those dreadful exceptions, stands forth one
of the noblest in human history.

His administration of the government, after he came to
the throne, was so wise, so able, so faithful, so conscientiously conformed to the divinely-given constitution of government, and withal so full of evidence of his honest and
affectionate regard for the welfare of his people, that inspiration has called him "a man after God's own heart," and
has regarded it as not dishonorable even to Messiah, to
make "Son of David" one of His most prominent desig-
nations.

The evident excellencies of David's administration could
hardly be more expressively set forth in so brief a summa-

ry, than they are in the text: "So he fed them according to the integrity of his heart; and guided them by the skill-fulness of his hands."

The pregnant significance of the word "fed" arises from its allusion to the humble labor of his early life, the care of sheep, so graphically described in the preceding verses, in which the writer does not fail to call our attention, by the most signal and touching instance of it, to that consid-erate and tender carefulness which so gracefully adorns the rugged strength of the manliest character, and which is so needful alike in the humble guardian of a flock and the supreme ruler of a people; the influence of which descends so sweetly and so benignly from the lofty summit of power into the low vales of society; floats over the land in all its breezes; tempers (without abating) the valor of its men; and covers with beneficent protection its women, its chil-dren, and its homes.

The Psalmist emphasizes, in his description of David's reign, the "integrity of his heart" and the "skillfulness of his hands"—not undervaluing (you see) that tact, that fertility of resources, that executive ability, that political wisdom, for which a ruler has so much occasion; yet exalt-ing to its due pre-eminence "integrity of heart," upright, uncorrupt, honest purpose.

If President Lincoln had lived to fulfill his second term of administration as worthily as he did the first; if then retiring from that high seat and from all public employ-ment, he had lived to a good old age among you, his neigh-bors and friends, and had here peacefully died, there is no need of doubting, no propriety in seeming to doubt, that those pages of history on which his name would have been written, would not only have contained the record of one of the most eventful periods, but the biography of one of the most blameless and one of the most illustrious of civil rulers; one to whom God had given a "skillfulness of hands" adequate to the necessities of a government struggling through extremest difficulties and dangers, and an "integrity of heart" which secured, by simply deserving it, that implicit confidence of a great nation, which, when given by a deceived people to the selfishly ambitious, furnishes the opportunity for establishing thrones of despotism amid the ruins of popular liberty.

The mournful premature ending of his noble career, the sudden and cruel snatching him from us by murderous violence, at the meridian of his official life, while it has filled the hearts of the people with unprecedented sorrow, does not diminish, (must it not deepen?) the reverent interest with which we meditate upon that character and that career. Has not God, in so fearfully smiting us, made all our hearts so tender, for this very purpose, that they may the more effectually receive the impressions which such meditation should make? "A glorious, beneficent gift of God has been withdrawn," said a venerable Christian orator,* to whom I listened on the day of President Lincoln's funeral obsequies at the National Capital, when all our hearts swelled and ached in the freshness of patriotic agony. It was not the language of extravagant eulogy, but the simple and sincere expression of candid Christian wisdom.

In this holy house, in which the honored dead used to worship, on the first Sabbath since we laid his reverend form in the grave, before "God who only is great," let our

*Rev. T. M. Post, D.D.

words and our thought be sober and temperate, even according to the good example so constantly set us by him of whom we are all thinking. Resting, according to the commandment, even from the labors of love and of filial grief, which, for more than half a month, have now occupied the minds and hands of the nation, let us devoutly meditate on that "glorious, benificent gift of God that has been withdrawn," endeavoring to fix in our minds the good lessons which we ought to learn, and so to secure the good and holy uses which God has kindly intended.

1. Let us reflect upon this, *that God, with merciful purpose toward our country, chose from the humble ranks of her people, the man who should be her ruler and savior, in the most perilous period of her history.*

I would not need to recount minutely the incidents of Mr. Lincoln's childhood and youth, even if I were prepared to do so, as I am not. I am speaking to that portion of his countrymen who least need such information. Sufficient for my purpose is the general fact, known to all men, that his early life was spent in rural situations and rustic employments, as much so as that of the son of Jesse. His social connections were as far from whatever would be deemed aristocratic, and his employments as remote from the splendors and the corruptions of cities. In both these men, as also quite as eminently in Washington, we have illustration of the great advantages of country life, for the rearing and education of useful and heroic men. In thus speaking, I do not disparage cities, nor deny their peculiar opportunities for developing character. I am happy to be increasingly convinced that the advantages for education and for

—2

happy and useful life, are not exclusively possessed by city or by country.

It is appropriate now, however, to note the value of country life and experience in the formation of character; and I think it evident that, in the case of the three historic characters just mentioned, the world is much indebted to the rustic experiences of their childhood and youth. Their rustic employments and sports were calculated to develop and strengthen their bodily powers, and to give them the physical hardiness and endurance for which they had so much need in subsequent life. This was not merely the power of enduring muscular exertion. For this the late President had not much occasion. He was not called, like Washington and David, to do military service in the field, and to undergo the personal physical privations and toils of warfare. But he was subjected to a continuous strain of mental exertion, and care, and solicitude, which tries the bodily powers even more severely than bodily toil and exposure. Probably no other man in our country has worked so hard and so steadily, during the last four years, as President Lincoln—no other brain has been subjected to so severe a pressure—no other human system has had its source of vitality, and its entire vital organization burthened with such a weight. We cannot well overrate the value to us, of that full and hearty respiration, that vigorous and even circulation, those steady nerves, those lithe, tough muscles, that hardy, robust frame, which had been secured, in so great degree, by the wholesome habits of his early life, and by those labors of which our western prairies, and forests, and rivers will for ages preserve the legends.

In this connection it should be noticed, that while Mr.

Lincoln came forth from among the humble and obscure, he did not come from among the degraded or vicious. Such constitutions as his are not the offspring of intemperance and debauchery, nor are they reared in squalid, and disorderly, and unhappy homes. Lowliness, obscurity, even poverty may consist with the strictest virtue and truest respectability. Preeminently is this so in our favored country; but it has been true, and illustrated by signal instances, in all countries and in all ages. A large proportion of the world's greatest men, the men whose lives have had the most decisive effects upon the world's history, rose from obscurity; had their childhood and youth amid humble scenes and surroundings; had their bodily and mental energies developed by vigorous labor, alternating with wholesome active sports, and free from the enervating influences of luxury. I have alluded to Washington, our great national example of heroic virtue. He was not indeed a child of poverty; and he was closely connected with what there was of aristocracy in those primitive days of our republic. But those were days, and that was an aristocracy, into which little of luxury entered. The habits and discipline and employments of Washington's early life were rugged and invigorating. The wealth and distinction of his kindred, and which he inherited, seem only to have added grace and dignity to the strength which frugal, and industrious, and temperate living gave him. And, notwithstanding his wealth and distinguished connections, his early orphanage, his limited literary advantages, his humble profession, and his manifest rising by his personal exertions and merits alone, constitute him as good an example as any of elevation from the ordinary ranks to the highest distinction.

Let it be attentively noted by the young, and by those whose greatest responsibility pertains to the rearing of the young, that God is apt to select His most honored human instruments from among the industrial classes—those who earn their living by labor; and that when one is chosen from among the wealthy, we find him to have been identified with those classes by voluntary industry, and frugality, and wise abstinence from luxury, showing that, whatever wealth he may have, he is not dependent upon it for ability to live well and happily; and that whatever position he may have by inheritance, is no higher than he might have attained by the fair exercise of his own powers.

President Lincoln's hardy and robust bodily frame was not the only good product of those early habits to which I have referred. His cheerful and hopeful temper have been and will continue to be celebrated. This doubtless had a close connection with his fine physical health. It largely resulted from those habits and exercises of his country life, which so admirably invigorated his body; and it is an occasion to us of gratitude to God, being one of the most important qualities of that "glorious and benificent gift" to our country and to mankind. I surely believe that his characteristic cheerfulness, his unfailing good humor, his hearty relish for the amusing, his ability to toss off from his aching shoulders the heavy burdens of care, responsibility and sorrow, and regale himself with hearty, boyish mirth, (always taking up again those burdens so quickly and bearing them so bravely and patiently), I surely believe that this was worth to the nation all that it was worth to preserve those noble powers, and prevent them from being long ago made to succumb and collapse.

Let the fastidious criticise his want of what they call dignity. Let the austere condemn what they call his vulgarity. Let them criticise the *turbidness* of the MISSISSIPPI. Let it be conceded (for I care little to investigate, whether it were actually so,) that his enjoyment of the ludicrous did sometimes carry him beyond the limits of perfect taste or perfect delicacy. We are not proposing to represent him as faultless. Let us thank God that the fault most proclaimed by his detractors, while it was possible for any to be such, was a fault so comparatively harmless, so consistent with the sterling honesty, the unsullied virtue, the exemplary temperance, the unquestioned purity, and the abundant kindness of heart, which all acknowledge. And now, when the voice of detraction is forever silent, let us acknowledge as a good gift of God, and a natural result of the wholesome habits of his early life, that "oil of gladness" which so kindly anointed our great defender, and spared his precious powers from the friction which else would have worn them swiftly out, making them creak in the harsh tones of tyrannic cruelty, or break into the discordant din of wild and ruinous phrensy.

11. Let us also reflect upon this: *That God did manifestly by His own Spirit, vouchsafe to that chosen man, a special divine preparation for his great work.*

That there is such a work of God's Spirit upon men chosen to eminent positions, distinct from that work on which the personal hope of eternal life depends, is clearly taught in scripture. Our text and its historical connection lead us to notice this in the case of David. When Samuel had anointed him in his father's house, "in the midst of his brethren," (as we read in 1 Sam. xvi: 13,) "the spirit of the Lord came upon David from that day forward." A similar statement is made concerning Saul, after his anointing, of which we have the account in the tenth chapter of the first book of Samuel. The sequel of his history does not permit us to believe that the Holy Spirit's effectual work of salvation was wrought upon Saul; and, although happily the contrary is true of David, I think we are warranted in regarding the declarations to which I have referred as denoting a work of special preparation for their public and official work, vouchsafed to them by the Spirit of God.

Surely, my brethren and my countrymen, we have abundant evidence of the same mercy having been shown to our late President and to us. How inevitably do your minds revert to that scene which probably many of you witnessed, at yonder railroad depot, in February, 1861, when the President-elect turned from the platform of the car which was to bear him hence to the national Capital, to say his simple farewell to you, his neighbors—a scene of most republican simplicity, yet none the less of historic grandeur, and of religious sublimity. You doubtless remember his touching allusions to all his life and experience among you—to his joys and successes, and his tender sorrows, which you had shared in neighborly sympathy. You remember the deep solemnity with which he adverted to the vast responsibilities he was about to assume, and the clear statement of his own deep conviction that his success depended absolutely on God's gracious help and blessing. You remember—yea, all the Christian world remembers—the simplicity and the unquestionable sincerity in which he closed that parting address with the request that you would pray for him. He spoke those simple words to you, his Springfield neighbors; but they were soon on the tremulous lips, under the moistening eyes, and in the thankful hearts of millions. From that time until the news of his murder was flashed abroad by the lightning, and wailed through all the air, and darkened all the land, it is probable that more prayer had continually been offered up to God for him, than for any one man who ever lived. In all sanctuaries in which loyal Americans worshiped; at all firesides where loyal households knelt; in all tents where devout soldiers have met for prayer; in all hospitals, where suffering patriots have languished, and Christian women have prosecuted their angelic ministration; at every picket station, where a Christian soldier has paced alone under the silent stars; in every chamber where a Christian woman has knelt in prayful remembrance of son, or husband, or brother, or lover; in myriads of cabins, where Christian slaves have waited for the coming of Him who proclaimeth "liberty to the captive;" beyond the seas, wherever our missionaries have gone to heathen or Mohammedan lands, or among the votaries of corrupt and paganized Christianity, and have gathered converts to simple and pure religion; wherever in Europe our cause has found Cobdens and Gasparins to make it understood, and honest lovers of popular liberty secured by constitutional government, to sympathize with our struggle; in the Pacific islands; in Southern and Western Africa; in the ports of China and Japan; in the great cities of India; amid the mountains of Persia; from the banks of the Tigris and Euphrates; in many provinces of Turkey; in Greece; in Italy, amid the Alpine heights; in every land where the

Gospel of Christ has made men free, or wakened within them prayerful and prophetic longings for freedom;—from all such lands, and from all such hearts, the prayer has gone up to God, which was asked for, in such simplicity, from that railroad platform in your city; and all those countless voices have linked with their prayers the name of ABRAHAM LINCOLN.

How clearly and how graciously has God answered those prayers! What a spirit of wisdom, and of patience, and of power did the Lord vouchsafe to him for whom they were offered! We make no claim for him of exemption from errors. He distinctly disclaimed all such preposterous pretensions. But, looking upon his administration, now closed, as a whole, I do not fear that any Christian man will doubt that he was signally guided and helped by God. That some of the most conspicuous and important acts of his administration were not contemplated when he took the reins of government, is certain. That he was led to them reluctantly by the providence of God shaping and moving the current of events on which he was borne, we have his frank avowal. That God accompanied the external indications and pressure of His providence with internal illumination and impulsion of His Spirit, I should deem it unscriptural to doubt. More sanguine and more impetuous men earlier urged some of the measures which he afterwards adopted; and if any think that this was by reason of greater sagacity and quicker insight than were given to the President, we will not dispute about that. Others may think that God mercifully saved us from the ruinous effects of rashness, by having formed the President's mind to careful and slow movement. Perhaps both classes will agree, that God's influence brought him to the adoption of those measures, not too soon, and not too late, to save the country—and in saving, to purify it from its greatest stain, and to deliver it from its greatest curse.

II. Let us, then, reflect upon *"the integrity of heart"* and *"skillfulness of hands"* with which our departed shepherd *"fed"* and *"guided"* us.

I desire to view these, and to speak of them, in Christian soberness, and in such temperate style as Mr. LINCOLN's discourses and writings so well exemplify.

The great eulogist of Washington, himself one of our most famous men, and who so lately ended his earthly life, in that patriotic discourse so many times delivered, alluded to the remark which had been made "that Washington was not a man of genius." Everett's reply was, that if one who accomplished what Washington did, (recapitulating his most illustrious achievements in a truly magnificent period which I cannot recite.)—if such an one were not a man of "genius," then "genius" is not an "indispensable' possession.

Can it be doubted that the most intelligent students of our country's history will form the same estimate of ABRAHAM LINCOLN? Doubtless more brilliant men than he have served the nation under his orders. Minds of more rapid movement, perhaps of greater comprehension, certainly of more varied and extensive learning, have aided his by their counsel. There have been emergencies in which the nation has been impatient of his slow deliberation; have murmured at his moderation; has been in agony of fear lest he should let the golden opportunity for its salvation

—3

pass irrecoverably by. But when he has made up his mind, when he has been ready to speak, how rarely has he failed to utter that which has commended itself to the best judgment of the people? When he has "set down his foot," how surely has it marked the ground on which the nation would thenceforth stand, the line from which the nation would never go back! And which of all her heroes or sages, not even excepting that first and greatest, has this nation more deliberately and more fully *trusted?* The ambitious may covet admiration—may be willing to be feared, if they can be applauded—but the highest earthly reward of true patriotism is a great people's *confidence*. This is indeed the best testimony to his "integrity of heart;" but not to that alone: a people whose political existence is in mortal peril do not entrust their supreme magistracy to one who is merely *honest*. They must believe that he is also *wise*. And, in such *deliberate* judgment, they are not *apt* to be mistaken.

Doubtless that, in respect to which President Lincoln's wisdom and integrity were most severely tried, and have been and will be most debated, is his treatment of the institution of slavery. He is accused, on the one hand, of having unconstitutionally directed the vast military power of the country against an institution of several States, which, under the constitution of the United States, they had a right to maintain. On the other hand, he is accused of having been slow and reluctant to embrace a glorious providential opportunity to rid his country of so great an evil, and to deliver millions of enslaved people and their offspring from cruel bondage. His own frank and lucid statements, and his most noted official acts, explaining and illustrating each other. show the following things, viz:

1. Mr. LINCOLN conscientiously regarded all chattel slavery as wrong, and sincerely desired that every human being might be free.

2. He did not regard the office of President of the United States as directly investing him with any authority to remedy that wrong. by setting free any human being who was held in slavery. As President of the United States in Washington, he did not understand himself as having any more right to abolish slavery in any State in which it existed, than he had had as simple Abraham Lincoln, Attorney and Counsellor at Law, in Springfield, Illinois; and he regarded his oath of office, as well as the general principles of morality, as forbidding him to usurp the smallest degree of unconstitutional power, for the sake of fulfilling his philanthropic desires.

3. He regarded his oath of office, and the fundamental principles of right which that oath sanctions, as binding him to defend and save the government which he was administering, at whatever cost to its assailants; and as he was ready, so far as they made it necessary, to destroy their lives by musketry and cannon, and to desolate their lands by war, in order to defeat their treasonable conspiracy and open rebellion; so, for the same purpose, it being justified by the same necessity, he was ready to emancipate their slaves: and when by the dreadful persistency of rebellion, it had been demonstrated that the continued existence of slavery is incompatible with the safety of the Union, he was ready to recommend to Congress and to the people that change in the Constitution, by which it is to be abolished and forever forbidden in all the land.

It were an idle speculation, to inquire whether possibly some other mind might have seen more quickly, and reasoned more acutely, and so have acted more promptly upon slavery's forfeiture of its constitutional guaranties, or whether one of such more rapid apprehension might with correspondingly greater rapidity have led the nation to the position which it did attain under President Lincoln's careful—if you please, even repressive—guidance. That were an idle speculation now, not only because it cannot now be applied for practical good, but because it could be only *speculation*, based upon *hypothesis*, not, like the historical judgment which is to be, upon *facts*. We cannot surely know whether all those *hypotheses* could have been made facts; nor whether the grand result, sought by more rapid methods, could have been reached at all.

Behold what is reached — the Union saved! the mightiest rebellion ever made against human government, utterly subdued! the arrogant slave-power which defied the world, humbled, not only, but crushed! four millions of bondmen liberated, and liberty assured to their posterity! the great Republic of the world redeemed from its great reproach, and shame, and consuming disease, and fitted to be the great exemplar and defender of regulated liberty for all mankind! These are the results which now, with humble yet firm assurance, we may claim that God has vouchsafed to us by that administration of our government to which He called, and for which He fitted ABRAHAM LINCOLN.

Standing near his fresh grave, preparing to erect a fit monument over it, could we wish for *facts* to be commemorated on that monument, better adapted to win from the millions who will visit it, a favorable judgment of "the integrity of his heart, and the skillfulness of his hands?"

Having distinctly alleged that a ruler may be the subject of a special work of God's Spirit, fitting him for his office, without experiencing that renewing work of the same divine Spirit on which personal salvation depends, and having claimed the former for our departed President, I cannot leave the theme without alluding to the question, full of so tender interest, whether he had that still more important experience which was just as necessary for him, in order to his salvation, as for any "publican or sinner." I understand that his name had never been enrolled on your list of communicants, and that he had never here been known as a professor of religion. But that he was an honest believer in not only theoretical, but experimental Christianity, is generally understood; and, without making more or less of the explicit professions of recent conversion which have been publicly reported of him, I may say that during the last two or three years, if not ever since his elevation to office, his published language and his public deportment have increasingly, and very decidedly impressed us as altogether becoming to a Christian. We believe that spiritual Christianity was an experience, a life, with him. So is our deep sorrow assuaged, not only by our thankful memories of his noble and useful career, and the great blessings to our country and to mankind, of which God made him the instrument but by the precious hope that he was a child of God, and an heir, through grace in Christ Jesus, of the bliss of Heaven,

THE FIT END OF TREASON.

2 Sam. xviii: 32.—"The enemies of my lord the king, and all that rise against thee to do thee hurt, be as that young man is."

You recognize these as the words of Cushi, a courier from that battle-field, on which Joab commanded the loyal forces of Israel, and on which the traitor Absalom was slain. Cushi has no farther place in the inspired record, than this brief account of his bearing to king David, from his chief officer in the field, tidings of the utter defeat of the rebellion, and the fit end of its gifted and unprincipled leader.

I ask you to notice two or three things, in this man who flits so swiftly across the historic scene, remaining only a moment in sight, yet in that moment revealing perhaps as much of his personal character, as would a swift runner, in dashing before you, of his graceful figure and agile limbs.

Notice his fine application of what had been at stake in the conflict between Joab and Absalom, and of the value of the result which had been achieved; notice his hearty and thorough loyalty; his sensibility in respect to the bereaved father; and the exceeding delicacy with which he made his communication, combining therein the admirable expression of his humane sympathy and of his steadfast loyalty.

Bringing his tidings of the rout and dispersion of the insurgent forces, he finds that as soon as the king's solicitude for his kingdom is relieved, the father's anxiety for his son breaks forth in the eager question, " Is the young man Absalom safe !" With self-control which is helped by his deep respect and sympathy, and with adroitness such as only fine sensibility gives, he avoids a direct answer, and shapes the form of his reply so as, if possible, to call up in David's mind, thoughts and emotions befitting the patriot and the king, and by which the agonizing grief of the father shall be held in abeyance. Without harshly asserting it, he reminds the king that Absalom has sunk the character of son in that of rebel and enemy; that he has endangered, not merely his father's person. but that civil authority of which that person is the " anointed" depository, and which was divinely given to protect and bless a great nation; and he intimates that, defeated in his infamous scheme by the valor and conduct of Joab and the loyal forces under him, the rebel has come to a fit end, an end fit for any who thus rise against a lawful and good government.

The text is an admirable example of that rhetorical force which, being unstudied, and resulting spontaneously from the appropriate state of a susceptible mind, utters in a few fit and capacious words, sentiments of far-reaching application, and of mighty power.

Although Cushi so properly refrained from telling king David what the fit fate of Absalom was, we have it graphically described in the context. His forces being utterly defeated in the battle, Absalom himself, mounted on a mule, probably fleeing for life, is most ignominiously caught by the boughs of an oak, entangling themselves in that abundant hair, in which he so foppishly gloried, and the animal escaping from beneath him, he dangles, helpless, in the air. This being reported to Joab, the sturdy warrior soon dispatches him, and wisely orders the slain carcass to be ignominiously buried, and a huge heap of stones to be piled upon it. In that miserable grave was buried, not only Absalom's body, but the traitor power which he had directed. This being done so vigorously by the military power under the rough but sagacious Joab, saved David from the fearful conflict between royal duty and paternal affection, and averted from the nation the peril which might thence have arisen.

Thoughts of the analogy between that rebellion which ended in the death of Absalom and of that which collapsed in the surrender of Lee, cannot to-day be new thoughts to you. All Bible-readers must have observed this analogy very frequently, during the progress of our war. The causelessness, the ingratitude, the falsehood, with which this rebellion was initiated, have reminded us of those of its ancient type; we have seen it progressing in similar perfidy and cruelty; and we have steadily expected for it a like ignominious end. Now, when the end has come, and we are witnessing its fit closing phenomena, I think that some reference to the analogy may help the meditations by which we try to secure to our minds the lessons which we ought to learn, and the influences which we need to feel, to fit us for our remaining duties. For this purpose, no servile attempt to trace the analogy through all possible, and to force it into impossible particularity will be made. I only bring the analogy to your recollection, in a general way, and ask you, under the influence of it, so far as it spontaneously af-

fects you, to consider the application to our own present
case of whatever applicable truth there is in those words
of Cushi, which I have taken for my text.

In doing this, it is fair to observe that we can claim the
infallibility of inspiration only for the *record* of Cushi's
words, not directly for the sentiment expressed in them.
We have no scriptural claim that he was an inspired man.
The scriptural truth of what he said must be judged by its
correspondence with the general tenor of the Bible, and the
specific instructions given in other parts of it. I choose
these words of Cushi, for my text, because they seem to
me to be a good expression of truth which pervades the
Bible; which is inwrought into the whole texture of its
morality and its theology; and which has a most important bearing upon the most practical questions with which
we now have to do. I would candidly leave all who hear
me to verify whatever I may say, by their own study of
the Bible, being quite sensible that, within the limits of
this discourse, I cannot expound, nor even cite all the
scripture which needs to be studied to this end. I must,
however, at this point, observe that I am not unmindful
of the impression on many minds, that the Christian pulpit
should hold forth none but the mild and winning aspects
of Bible-truth; that it should utter only messages of mercy;
that it properly has no ministry of terror and of wrath. I
have not, however, so learned the Gospel; have not so read
the Bible. My Bible has both Testaments in it; and I
yield not a moment to the assumption that the Old Testament is superceded by the New. The New Testament is a
divine commentary upon the Old; the Old Testament is
fully developed in the New. The Levitical ceremonial of
—4

the Old Testament has indeed given place to that scriptural worship which it symbolized, and which the New Testament more clearly fulfills; but the essential morality and the essential theology of the Old and New Testaments are one and the same. Again, the most terrific revelations of the divine wrath are made in the New Testament, in words which fell from the gracious lips of our Redeemer; and no Old Testament writer has more forcibly exhibited "the terror of the Lord," than the most voluminous writer of the New Testament.

Still further, the most particular instructions of the New Testament concerning civil government are given by Paul, who puts "*the sword*" into the ruler's hand; declares that he bears it "*not in vain*"—not as a mere unmeaning ornament, but to glitter with a keen and threatening edge; and he solemnly entitles him "the minister of God," "a revenger to execute wrath upon him that doeth evil."

That view of civil government which makes it a mere system of "moral suasion," and which proposes to accomplish its ends by conciliation alone, discarding coercion, and disclaiming all terror of penalties, is not the New Testament view. The civil ruler of the New Testament is armed with the sword.

I have thus stated to you, my friends, very briefly, the general views which appear to me, not only to justify, but to require the Christian pulpit to set forth clearly, with no uncertain sound, the religious obligations of this nation, in respect to the rebellion which is just now breaking down; in respect to the atrocities which have so fully revealed its enormous wickedness; in respect to the men upon whose souls is the guilt of it; and in respect to that system of slavery from which it derived its life and its malignity.

THE FIT END OF TREASON is, then, the theme upon which I address you. On Thursday last, we closed in yonder cemetery, a funeral service of fifteen days' continuance. A funeral procession which had solemnly moved from the national capital, by a route of some 1500 miles, through many of the States, pausing at many of the chief cities, and all the way attended by the reverent, tearful salutations of the thronging people, then and there reached its destination. We laid in that sepulchre that form on which it was truly observed that more weeping eyes had looked than probably upon any human form ever extended in death before. Why was it? Was it that Abraham Lincoln was absolutely the greatest and best man who ever lived? Probably none of us are prepared to affirm quite so much; and if any were—even if this were unquestionably true—we should not in this alone have the full explanation of what we have witnessed and experienced. Our mourning has regard to his official and representative character. We mourn not merely, not mainly, for the man, but for the President—not merely for the kind and just, the good and great man, but for the worthy, the elect, the consecrated RULER. He was to us "the Lord's anointed." His sudden death was the sudden demolition of the precious casket in which all the majesty and all the sacredness of supreme magistracy were enshrined. He had not only died, but had been murdered—cruelly, treacherously, basely murdered. Our horror of that murder was not merely for it as the murder of a fellow-man; we knew that the blow was struck at him in his official and representative capacity. The murder meant the ruler, not the man. The murderer would far

more gladly have made the nation his victim, would far
more gladly have destroyed the government of which Mr.
Lincoln was the head. That murder did thus concen-
trate in itself and did thus fitly represent the baseness, the
treachery, the malignity, the desperateness, the murderous
malice of that rebellion by whose ideas it was inspired, in
behalf of which it was plotted, and in the interest of which
it was accomplished.

That miserable stage-player,* accustomed to act tragic
scenes, morbidly brooding over those dark plots and des-
perate actions which form so large a part of the material
of his trade, aspiring to the fame of pre-eminence in crime,
fooled probably by dreams suggested by a name of historic
and tragic eminence in his family, heartily sympathizing
with the great conspiracy against the noble government,
whose protection he still accepted and enjoyed, accomplished the premeditated murder successfully. He fled
from the scene of it, and for twelve days eluded the aven-
gers of blood—twelve days of bodily torture, from that
bruised limb which the finger of divine Providence so sea-
sonably touched, and just enough disabled—twelve days,
no doubt, of mental misery far more severe. Then over-
taken, discovered in ignominious concealment, summoned
to surrender himself to justice, but refusing, knowing too
well what justice was, burned out as a ferocious beast
might be, shot in his movement to escape, by the faithful

---

*I cannot but think that Booth was a fit instrument for the assassination of the
President, and trained in a fit school; for although some good men do strangely
consent to seek relaxation in the theatre, and although I do not question what is
alleged of the good character of Edwin Booth, and of *some other* actors, who
seem to be regarded as *exceptiona*, I am sure that no other profession is so well
adapted to produce just such a character as J. Wilkes Booth, or to qualify him
to relish and to plan, and to perpetrate just such a crime.

soldier, but whose bullet, God, in marvelous exactness
of retribution, guided to his brain, the wretched murderer met the death he so much merited, and missed
the gratification which, I have no doubt, he would have
experienced, in being the principal figure in another
tragic scene, swelling again in theatric pomp before the
court which would have sentenced him to the gallows. A
wise and vigorous administration takes care that he shall
have no grave on which either the wicked sympathy of
treason or the weakness of natural affection, (which the
nation pities but must not gratify,) nor yet the morbid silli-
ness of sentimentality can ever shed its tears. The faithful vigilance of our rulers has caused the arrest of several
other persons accused or suspected of complicity with this
dreadful crime. We must not forget that due vigilance re-
quires the arrest of all to whom any reasonable suspicion
attaches, and therefore, is likely to occasion the arrest of
numbers who will not be proved guilty—probably of some
who are, and will be found entirely innocent. Let any
such bear the hardship patiently, and let us be ready to
show them all proper sympathy. But if any are indeed
guilty, and God shall, in His providence, enable our government to make their guilt appear, let them share the fate of
him in whose crime they have participated.

On the very day on which we followed the body of our
lamented President to its honored burial, we read the proc-
lamation of his successor, announcing the possession by the
government of evidence that justifies the charge of complicity in this crime against Jefferson Davis and five others,
some of whom have held high places in the government
against which they have been in rebellion. The President

also offers large rewards for their arrest, in order to their arraignment for trial. If he who has been the chosen head of the rebel power, to crush which has cost the nation so much, is guilty of this murder, and shall be brought into the power of the government, that guilt being made to appear, I presume that no voice will be raised to plead for him against the ignominious fate to which he will doubtless then be doomed. But suppose that he shall not be proved to have been the employer or instigator of the assassin, nor to have been privy to his crime, nor to have approved it— what then? Of what do we and all mankind already know Jefferson Davis to be guilty, beyond all need of proof, and all possibility of denial? Is it not exactly the same offense for which Absalom died, and by which his name is blackened with peculiar infamy? Davis has been far more successful than Absalom. We had no Joab ready, in the beginning, to direct the martial movements which would bring upon the conspiracy so swift defeat. He to whom we looked for this, who had so long and so prosperously led the national armies, had become an old man, feeble and broken, and in the very hour of her supremest need and danger, the country found herself called to gently and reverently provide for her aged hero's retirement, and then address herself to the task of finding or training competent leaders for her eager, multitudinous, but yet untrained hosts of volunteer soldiers. For, alas! he who next to the aged Scott, was best fitted by education and experience, for that noble leadership, educated at the national military school, already honored in the national service, a native and resident of the same State of which Scott and Washington were natives, inheriting a portion of Washington's wealth, and having the prestige of affinity with Washington's family, closed his ears against the patriotic warnings of Scott; trampled under his feet the principles of Washington; forsook the counsels and examples of those early Virginians whose wisdom and patriotism gave their native State so glorious a share in founding the republic; and, with a folly like Rehoboam's, followed the guidance of those "architects of ruin" who had obtained political control of degenerate Virginia, and made her pestilent heresy of State sovereignty the plausible apology for rebellion. Col. Robert E. Lee—(he never has received any higher rank from any government that now exists, or that ever had a right to exist)—Col. Robert E. Lee, of the United States Army, very deliberately resigned his honorable rank and position when his country needed his services, and gave his services, his education, his talents, his sword—to "Virginia," he says. Yes, to Virginia in rebellion, and to all who would combine with Virginia in her rebellion. Let him look to Virginia for suitable reward of the service he has rendered her.

Col. Lee's defection prevented the early defeat, and rendered possible the temporary success and the endurance through four terrible years, of that rebel power of which Jefferson Davis was the head. That power is now destroyed. Davis is now a fugitive from justice. It is the duty of all good citizens to seize him, if possible, and deliver him to the government. If this shall be done, or if in resisting the attempt to do this, he shall share the fate of Booth, or of Absalom, what impartial reader of history will say that he is less deserving of it than they? Waiving all question of his direct complicity with Booth, or his knowledge of his purpose, who will be able to separate in thought the murder of the President, from Davis' persistent effort to murder the Union? Who possibly can think that Booth hated the President for anything else than for his faithful and successful defense of the Union against Jefferson Davis? Who can doubt to whose protection the murderer was sagaciously flying? Who doubts that if he could have slain his victim and escaped to Richmond, while Davis still ruled there, he would have received the honors and applauses for which he morbidly thirsted? What possibility is left to us, by the careful, abundant, published testimony, of doubting that thousands of as innocent and patriotic men as Abraham Lincoln, have deliberately been *starved to death*, by the authority of Jefferson Davis, and without one word of remonstrance from Robert E. Lee?

These kindred crimes, (starvation of helpless prisoners to weaken the loyal army, and assassination of the President, to distract or paralyze the nation,) must be admitted to indicate the nature of that rebellion, in whose interest and by whose inspiration they have been committed. They are symptoms of its malignity; they are illustrations of its barbarity; and they are least surprising to those who have longest and most carefully studied that system in behalf of which this great rebellion was made. The barbarities of rebel prisons, during the last four years, are not more dreadful than the customary, legalized practices of that domestic slave trade of which Richmond was long the most famous mart.

I have heard a man of the highest respectability describe a scene which his own eyes had witnessed in that city — a large company of little children, neatly and even gaily dressed, ready to be sold at auction, each to the highest bidder; and we know that, daily, in those slave-markets, children, and men, and women were placed upon the auction block for sale. Their muscles, their bones, their bodily vigor, their brains, their intelligence, their beauty, their modesty, their virtue, their piety—all were articles of sale or qualities determining their market value.

The number of little children who have been torn from their mothers to be sold in Richmond, into regions from which those mothers would never hear from them again— the number of adult men similarly sold away from their families—the number of adult women (*some* of whom were as modest and as fair as our own sisters or daughters,) who have stood on those auction-blocks, exposed to sale to the highest bidder, without question of his purposes and without defense against his will—of either of these, I think it not unlikely, in all the years while those horrors were legalized, the number may have been greater than the whole number of our men ever confined in the prisons of Richmond. Yet, which of us would not prefer all the horrors of such imprisonment to the experience in his own person or that of child or sister, of that one incident of slavery?—an incident, however, which only fairly illustrates the nature, and laws and principles of that accursed institution.

That *that* instsiution might be made the foundation of a new empire, which should encircle the Gulf of Mexico as the Roman Empire did the Mediterranean, and should dominate this continent as that did the other, was the purpose of that rebellion which Jefferson Davis led, and to which Alexander Stephens adhered after publishing to the
—5

world a clear and unanswerable refutation of all the political pretexts on which its early advocates sought to justify it. Our government does not need, scarcely can it have a more complete justification of its firm stand against that rebellion, and its final complete subjugation of it, than the simple transcript upon the historic page of that famous speech against secession, made and published by Alexander Stephens, a few weeks before he became "Vice President" of the rebel confederacy.

Is there wanting, in the falsehood of its inception, in the ungodliness of its principles, in the inhumanity of its purpose, or in the fiendish malignity of its deliberately chosen methods, anything to render this great rebellion detestable and deserving of as ignominious an end as that of Absalom's rebellion?

In respect to the duty of our government to inflict judicial vengeance upon the leaders or adherents of rebellion, as such, irrespective of their direct complicity in the crime of assassinating the President, I am not disposed to dogmatize. There are questions of law and right on that subject upon which I prefer to await the investigation and decision of the proper tribunals. The former experience of our country has been so happy that we have had little occasion to study many of these questions.

The question (for example) what are the legal liabilities of men whose surrender has been accepted as prisoners of war, and who faithfully keep their parole, is one which seems to me to be overlooked by some who demand without qualification, that men who are in that situation, shall be put to death.

I do not discuss that question. Let it be discussed by

the lawyers,* and decided by the courts. But it is proper here to exhort all to cultivate careful and scrupulous regard for all the obligations of veracity and honor which
shall be found to exist. If, according to the true principles
which should govern in the case, as expounded by those
who are competent to expound them; if, according to the
laws and usages of Christian nations, the faith of our country is properly to be regarded as pledged to Lee and John-
ston, and all who were surrendered under them, let that
faith be kept carefully, scrupulously. Let not a hair on
the head of one of them be touched, contrary to any
pledge which lawfully commits and binds the government.

Let the like carefulness and scrupulousness apply, according to the facts and laws that are applicable to the
case of Davis,† or Breckenridge, or Stephens, or any other
one whom our government may have in its power.

Let us carefully, prayerfully guard ourselves against all
the natural tendency of our minds to feelings of revenge.
No personal bitterness or malignity is justifiable. But it is
not personal bitterness nor malignity which most firmly

*Professional opinions and expositions of the law which the writer has more
recently seen, convince him that the military parole does not release men from
responsibility to the courts for any belligerent acts in violation of the laws of
war, (e. g. murder and starvation of prisoners,) nor for their original crime of
treason. The degree of executive clemency to be exercised is a question for the
President. May God give him wisdom and firmness to be neither unnecessarily
severe, nor so merciful to criminals as to be "cruel the nation."

†Since this discourse was delivered and before it goes to press, we are permitted to rejoice that the official head of the conspiracy has been *arrested*—that he
is in the power of the government *as an arrested criminal*, caught in disguise,
not surrendered with an army, under military capitulation—and that whatever questions there may be about such capitulations, they can in no wise
apply to him.

Col. R. E. Lee has been reported as pleading for his late master in crime, that
he (Davis) no more deserves punishment than any who acted under him. "He
was only the *representative* of those who accepted his control in their organized

and most sternly demands the due punishment of treason. There is no inconsistency between the touching exhortation to "charity for all" and "malice toward none," with which our late President closed his last inaugural address, and the declarations of the present President, that mercy to individuals may be cruelty to the nation, and that it is necessary for the safety and peace of the nation, and of coming generations, that treason be recognized and treated as an infamous crime.

I remember no finer discrimination than that which was once made by Daniel Webster, in regard to the object of penal law. The counsel for the defense of a person accused of a crime, (Webster being counsel for the prosecution,) had said in his plea. "The object of the law is not to punish the guilty, but to protect the innocent." Webster's clear logic detected, and his powerful rhetoric exposed the fallacy by this reply: "The object of the law is to protect the innocent *by* punishing the guilty."

Under the influence of Christian sentiments, we did not desire, *as an end*, that even the murderer of our President should be put to death, but we did desire it as the means to an end, an end for which the lives of ten thousand such as he might well be given. We would fain make the murder of this nation's President, the sacrilegious violation of the

rebellion." Very well. We accept this view. Davis was no more *guilty* than many others—but he and they consented that he should be their "*representative*." As their representative he has been arrested; as their representative let him suffer the full penalty of the law. As lovers of justice, and still desiring the least shedding of blood which will answer the ends of justice, we devoutly thank God that he has given into the power of our rulers the one man, who more fitly than all others, may "*represent*" the great rebellion *to the end*. And when he shall have fulfilled his *representative* obligation as he is now likely to do, "let all the people say *Amen*."

nation's highest authority, an impossible crime—a crime to which hereafter no wretch will dare to be tempted.

In like manner would we, if possible, secure the coming generations of this people against the danger of such a conspiracy as it has cost this generation so much of its blood to quell. No life that has been forfeited to justice should be spared from considerations of mercy, to the diminishing of that security. Yet, let us not suppose that our security depends entirely upon the bringing to justice of the leaders of rebellion. Or rather, let us not suppose that their arraignment and trial before our courts is the only method by which, in God's righteous providence, they may be brought to justice. If they escape to foreign lands, as Arnold did, and know that they can never return to their native land, save to be arrested as felons—if any of them are permitted to live, disfranchised, amid constituents whom they have ruined—will they not dolefully sigh, as Cain, "My punishment is greater than I can bear?" Will not their blighted reputations, and the ever-increasing ignominy of that detestable cause to which they sacrificed their positions and characters, be the most effectual warning to the young men in the future? And is not the woe and desolation which their chosen war has brought down upon the rebel communities, a retribution and a warning of the same import and effect, as any judicial inflictions could be, and on a far grander scale?

Behold the devastation of fields, and the desolation of cities, through all the rebel States! Their homes are all dark with a sorrow which no joy of victory can lighten. Their women are all dressed in mourning for men buried in graves which shall have no honorable monuments. The maimed and crippled survivors of their conquered armies can have no honoring pensions. We will feed them in charity, but they can aspire to no higher *honor* than *pardon* and *amnesty!* And even their innocent orphans—our care must be not to remind them of their parentage. O, this has been the crime of States, and on the whole people of those States must inevitably come the just, the exemplary, the monitory punishment. This, it is now abundantly manifest, God has appointed—this in His wonderful providence, He is fearfully executing. Let us be content to be merely instruments in His hands, and submissive also to our share of the judgment, for sins in which our late President so solemnly reminded us that both parts of the nation have participated.*

And finally, humbly sensible of our fallibility, and the fallibility of our rulers, let us fervently pray God to keep us, and to guide and uphold them. Turning away from the grave of our murdered President, of which you, the people of Springfield, and your children after you, are to be the favored custodians, let us give to his lawful successor our prayers, and our vows, and our sustaining sympathy. May God make him so wise, and faithful and strong, and enable him so to illustrate his country's justice that all her loyal people shall dwell in safety and peace, because all who would rise against her to do her hurt, shall have rea-

---

*Slavery was the Absalom of this rebellion, the parricide of our country. It has thrust its shaggy head into the stiff boughs of the good old oak of Union; the miserable mule of secession that it rode has slipped away from beneath it, and left it dangling; its heart is pierced by the "three darts" of confiscation, presidential emancipation and the employment of freedmen as soldiers; and now behold the people piling upon its carcass, like a "very great heap of stones," their State ordinances of abolition and the National Constitutional Amendment, which is to "proclaim liberty throughout all the land, unto *all the inhabitants thereof.*"

son to expect a fate as fearful and as ignominious as that of Booth and of Absalom.